For Mary Wolf and Kathy Schenck—
in all the universe there are no better friends

C. L.

For Eitan T., whose spirit is higher than the
moon and brighter than the stars. With love,

O. E.

Library of Congress Cataloging-in-Publication Data
Loomis, Christine. Astro Bunnies / Christine Loomis ; pictures by Ora Eitan. p. cm.
SUMMARY: Astro Bunnies take rockets into space, explore, and return home.
I. Eitan, Ora, 1960– ill. II. Title. PZ8.3.L8619 As 1999
[E]—dc21   97-6893 CIP AC
ISBN 0-399-23175-7
1 3 5 7 9 10 8 6 4 2
First Impression

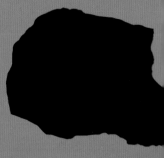

Astro Bunnies

CHRISTINE LOOMIS

Pictures by **ORA EITAN**

G. P. Putnam's Sons · New York

Astro bunnies
See a star
Think they'd like to
Go that far

Slip on silver
Suits with pockets
Climb up stairs
To shiny rockets

Rockets stand so
Straight and tall
Bunnies on the ground
Look small

Push a button
Twist a dial
Rocket launches
Bunnies smile

Zip and zoom
Up through the sky
Astro bunnies
Wave good-bye

Whiz and whoosh
The rocket races
Through the deep
And darkened spaces

Over Venus
Under Mars
Bunnies follow
Shooting stars

Sagittarius

Astro bunnies
Unsnap straps
Open hatches
Ports and flaps

Roll up, float up
Through the air
Stroll up, bounce up
Everywhere

Astro bunnies
Work together
Measure comets
Chart the weather

Gather moondust
From a crater
Scientists can
Study later

Ride their rockets
In slow motion
Through a silent
Starry ocean

Gliding by
The Milky Way
Where night is dark
And so is day

Then a ship
Appears in space
Bunnies from
Another place!

Astro bunnies
Love exploring
Making new friends
Scouting, touring

Yet wherever
Bunnies go
There is one thing
They all know

Rockets fly and
Rockets roam
But bunnies ALWAYS
Come back home